Seasons

Written by Amy White

Do you like spring?
Birds sing in spring.

You do not need a hat.
You can play with a ball and bat.

April showers bring May flowers.

Spring is yellow, red, and blue.
It is green, orange, and purple, too!

Do you like summer?
It is hot in the summer.

You can swim all day.

Let's run around. It's time to play!

In summer, fireflies take flight.
They light up the night.

Summer is time to eat outside.
Pack a basket and go for a ride!

Do you like autumn?

Leaves change colors in autumn.

Maybe you say autumn or maybe you say fall.
Quick, get out the soccer ball!

In autumn, it's time to rake leaves.
You can jump in the pile, if you please.

Do you like winter?
It is colder in winter.

In winter, you need a coat and hat.
Wipe your boots on the front mat.

When there is snow,
look how fast you can go!

winter

spring

summer

autumn

Which season do you like the best?